WINGS

BOOK ONE

ME, WITH WINGS

A STORY BY PHEONIX

Dedicated to God
He gave me the dream

READER COMMENTARY

I couldn't put it down. The story was so
exciting - dinner had to wait!

Grandma Joan, Canton, MI

Gripping story. Goosebumps covered my skin as
I eagerly dived into Pheonix's world.

Jennifer, Ann Arbor, MI

That was the best book ever! I loved it!

Faith, 9 yrs, Ann Arbor, MI

PREFACE

I live in a place where nobody knows my secrets except myself, sometimes my mom, and now you. My street is called Timber Street. It's very long, and only a few families live along it. We've all adopted tree names. My last name is Pine, and we live about a quarter mile up the road from our closest neighbors, the Maples. They have three kids who speak French like their dad.

About a mile down the road live our second-closest neighbors, the Spruces. We hardly ever see them, except on Sunday when we all go to church. The Spruces have four kids, two dogs, two cats, and a HUGE house. Across the road and about a half mile down live The Aspens, with two kids.

Five miles up the road live a family that is kind of remote. They have about three hundred acres of land and prickly, thorny brambles surrounding their home. They come to church, just two adults, and they're really nice but a little shy. Their last name is Birch. Then two-thirds-of-a-mile up the road live The Oaks. They have two teenage kids who are awesome, but we don't see them very often.

In my immediate family there are six kids - well, three are over twenty years old, but my brother and I are 7 and 11. We also have an adorable nephew who's only four: he's the son of our youngest older sister. Kinda confusing, but oh well. Anyway, what was I gonna tell you? Oh, yeah. Welcome to the Preface. Next comes....

CHAPTER ONE

This all started when I hugged something..... I don't remember what it was now, but I know I hugged it too long. That was back when I was four. I remember mom and dad telling me in nervous voices to let it go, and I remember wondering why.... but that's it. From then on, my back's been aching and mom and dad have been keeping some sort of secret from me. I used to hate it, but over the years I've gotten used to both things.

I walked through the woods, alone. I just felt the urge to breathe fresh oxygen, so I got permission to go for a walk.

For whatever reason, my back was aching more than usual that day.

I walked along, minding my own business, when – poof! - the earth gave way beneath my feet and I tumbled into a wide, shallow pit. It was full of flowers. I gasped and smiled. This would fill my dried flowers journal to bursting! But then an odd feeling came. I no longer wanted to pick the flowers. I got up and went back the way I came - I had walked long enough.

When I got back to the house, I went into my room, where my crafting supplies were. I took out my easel, paints and brushes, and let my heart guide my hands. Bright and mellow colors swirled on the paper, merging but not muddling. I loved this. It was a beautiful feeling. I closed my eyes and painted. My hand stopped when there was a knock on the door. I opened my eyes, surveying my work and said, without turning around, "Come in."

In came mom. "Honey, lunch should be ready in a few minutes. Start cleani - " she stopped talking abruptly. I could feel her eyes rest on my back. Confused, I turned around to face her. Her mouth was a thin line and her eyes were worried. "We need to talk."

Thoroughly worried and confused, I followed her down two flights of stairs. I knew the basement through and through, and wondered where she was taking me. She went into the off-limits room, motioning to me to follow when I hesitated. I had been in this

3

room many times, despite its off-limitness, and wondered if she knew.

She headed for the odds-and-ends shelf, full of large paint buckets, huge paint brushes that were probably used when the house was first decorated, Mom and Dad's old baby toys, mounds of metal tags - dog tags, collected over many generations.

There were more items on that shelf that I longed to explore, but mom was waiting for me so I wrenched my gaze away. She was focused on a small, flat, green thing, which I assumed was a piece of dried playdough and wondered why mom was so interested in it.

She reached out and tapped it. I stifled a yelp as the cabinet slid sideways, revealing a dark passageway. The "ceiling" overhead was thumped loudly and two pairs of running feet came down the steps. Dad and Bendo, my brother, appeared beside us, both panting.

We walked quickly down the passage, which lit up as soon as our feet touched the floor. We walked along the twisting route for some time before it widened and opened to a small underground cave. A few families from Timber were already in the cave, a bit out of breath. Others were coming in through more passages in the walls of the cave. Soon everyone on the street was there.

Mom instructed me to sit on one of the small boulders along the cave wall, facing toward the middle. I leaned against the rock wall but flinched and sat up straight as my back touched the cold surface. Mom sat beside me, as there was room for two.

After the Timber Street residents had been seated, another head peeked out of a smaller passage that nobody had noticed. It was an unfamiliar head, with plain-looking brown hair and freckles. A slim, small figure crept out. She looked about my age. Carefully keeping her back out of sight, she sat on the dirt floor. After a long silence, mom looked at each person in turn, very seriously.

"Most of you remember my daughter's incident some years back." There were nods from the people older than me and worried or confused looks from those younger or the same age as me.

"Well, lately her back has been aching and I've noticed a.... a....... *something* on her back."

The cave erupted in murmurs and whispers. I caught the words, "Impossible!", "It's only a myth," and "Worst fears" before mom quieted them.

"Please, please! They're only tiny! Quiet down!"

What was '*only tiny?*' I was *really* worried now. The brown-haired girl's eyes widened and she stared at me.

"Will Conderen please come forward?"

The cave was still for a long second, then the girl came forward, edging around the rock wall with her back out of sight.

"Conderen, will you teach Pheonix, please?"

Conderen nodded shyly.

"Thank you. Let us go to our homes - but Conderen, would you please come to our house?"

We left along with everybody else. Conderen followed, walking backwards until we went around a bend and couldn't see the cave anymore. I wondered why she didn't like people seeing her back. Once I looked back to see if she was still following - her footsteps were so soft - and I did a double-take. I could have sworn I'd seen a short, gauzy sheet streaming behind Conderen.

Chapter Two

I had a talk with Conderen when we got back in my room. She surprised me by asking if I had wings. I answered honestly, "No, of course not," and she told me to look over my shoulder. My shirt was sticking away from my back like it was being pushed out from the inside by two sticks.

I was speechless. My mouth opened and closed again and again, but no sound came out. Finally I managed to squeak, "I have *wings*?!"

Conderen nodded, smiling. "You probably don't remember me," she said, "but I hugged a kinzi's egg when I was only four and a half. You followed my example, and it turned us both half kinzi."

Seeing the confused expression on my face, she explained: "A kinzi is a type of shape-shifter. Most kinzies have limited shapes, but the kinzi who laid the egg that we hugged was a kinzi that could turn into anything. As we get older, we'll be able to control the kinzi half of us more."

I was still confused, but I nodded numbly.

She seemed pleased, and she smiled. It lit up her whole face, which had seemed even a bit hostile before, but which was now transformed to a point of irresistibleness.

To my surprise, she started to take off her shirt, but I soon saw that she had a white undershirt on beneath it. Slowly, so as not to surprise me too much, she unfolded a pair of two-foot-long wings. I gasped. My shirt was tight against my chest and I longed to take it off.

I climbed out of my loft, got a white undershirt and some scissors. I cut two slits in the back of the shirt, then went into the bathroom to try it on. I slipped the wings into the slits and was surprised to feel them tingle, as though they were asleep.

It wasn't so much the tingling that surprised me so much as the fact that I could *feel* the wings. The top ones were about six inches long, the bottom pair was about one and a half. They were a see-through white, the veins traced with glimmering rainbows. They were beautiful. They made an almost crinkling noise when they were bent, like cellophane only less sharp.

I went back into my room to find Conderen waiting for me. I climbed up to my bed.

"Pheonix, have you ever tried to make something just by thinking?"

"No."

"Well, will you do me a favor?"

"Sure....I guess."

"Picture a button in your mind while holding out your hands."

I closed my eyes and did as she said, picturing a little white button. A smooth surface tapped my hand. I opened my eyes instinctively to see a small, white button like the one I had pictured. My first thought was that Conderen had put it there, but no; she could not have known what I had pictured.

Conderen was beaming. "First try: perfect! The first time I tried that, I got a chunk of coal."

"A chunk of coal?!"

"Yup! I wanted a shiny black, square button. Guess I jumped in too far too early. Add on detail slowly; say a few words to describe the object, then the name of the object while picturing it. If you get really good, you can picture it, and not have to describe it!"

"Cool. Where did you learn to do this?"

"The egg talked to me."

" *Talked* to you?!"

"Yup. You can make other stuff too, you know."

"Really?"

"Yup."

"Cool!"

"Yup."

I thought about it, and decided to make a force field. I pictured a small bubble, like a soap bubble. I held out my hand, waited a little, and opened my eyes. There in my hand, feather-light and seeming almost to glow, was a blue-tinted force field about the size of a tennis ball.

I heard Conderen gasp. Looking up, I saw Conderen staring in admiration at the force field. After a moment she looked up. "I can only make one the size of an acorn," she said. I closed my hand around the blue sphere. "Can I make things disappear?"

"Yup."

"How?"

"Just picture the thing vanishing."

"It's that easy?!"

"Yup."

"Cool!"

"Yup."

CHAPTER THREE

I sat up and stretched. Looking around, I gasped. The walls of my room were painted just like a forest. Thick, green, grass-like carpet covered the floor, blotched in some places by short, dark green moss-like carpet. Suddenly the dream of last night rushed back to me - I had been dreaming my room looked just like this, I pictured it exactly.

I was amazed. I had just pictured this room – in my *sleep* - and it appeared! Conderen rolled over, looked around her and sat straight up. "Pheonix!" she screeched. Her wings stood straight up from surprise and excitement. "Do you know what this means?!?!"

"No," I replied honestly.

Hesitating, she slowly spoke: "You *may* be able to use other kinzi powers."

I nearly screamed. I nearly cried. I nearly hit my head on the ceiling. I nearly flew. Huh?

"OH. MY. GOSH," I said. My heart pounded and I got major goose bumps. Very slowly, I turned my head around to look behind me. Pointing toward the sky, on *my* back, were a pair of ten-foot-long wings, identical to my previous ones, only extremely huger.

I wondered if I could control these gigantic new additions to my anatomy. I experimentally flexed each muscle that I could possibly move voluntarily, starting with my forehead (eyebrows) and moving down.

Right under my shoulder blades were eight new muscles: two for each individual wing.

I gently tested each in turn, finding that I could move the additional limbs fairly accurately - I could even curl them up or fold them without fingering them. I started to call mom, but thought better of it and turned to Conderen instead, who had taken out a little comb from a pouch in her pocket and was ordering her hair.

I went to the dresser next to my bed and took my brush from on top of it.

All of that day I prepared to show my parents my wings, hiding them folded up beneath my shirt.

Chapter Four

The next morning I awoke in utmost excitement. Climbing down from my bed, I woke up Conderen who was sleeping on the thickly carpeted floor, her head on a pillow I had found in the linen closet. I shook her and she groaned and rolled away from me, covering her head with her pillow.

I grabbed the pillow and tried to wrestle it from her grasp, but succeeded only in shooting backwards and hitting my head on my bed.

Ouch.

Suddenly I had an idea. I stalked to Conderen's side, placed my hand on the pillow, and imagined it vanishing. Immediately the pillow disappeared. Conderen sat up and stared at me in amazement, than a smile spread itself over her face. Pleased, I smiled back.

We combed our hair and went downstairs - Conderen had an idea. We went outside and I climbed the apple tree behind the house. I spread my wings, jumped, and plummeted straight down. I was prepared. I landed on my feet, my hands hitting the ground just a moment later.

Climbing the tree again, I gave a few practice flaps with my wings. The pressure of my feet against the tree decreased visibly. I jumped, pumping my wings, and drifted slowly toward the ground at about the rate of speed of a slightly deflated balloon. I landed with a soft thump. The wind in my wings felt wonderful, but there was no fence around our yard and I didn't want anybody to see me besides my parents and brother. I then told Conderen my suspicions.

"Conderen?"

"Yup?"

"Well...... I have an idea......"

"Yup?"

"I think the more I use my powers, especially in large form, the bigger my wings and powers get - a bit more major use and I *may* be able to change form - when my wings are fully grown."

"Wow. I'd like to see *that*!"

"Okay.... I'll try to make a......... tree appear."

I held out both hands and pictured a Pine, my namesake, in our yard. A tiny rumble quivered through the earth and suddenly there was an almost full-grown pine tree, like the one I had pictured, in the backyard of the Pine residence. I looked behind me to see my wings tremble and grow three feet.

Then, everything disappeared and I was pitched, it seemed, into another world. It was full of flowers, like the ditch I had found on my walk through the woods only yesterday, only this flower-place had a statue of a dragon with huge wings and a webbed frill along its neck and back. It was up on its hind legs, its mouth open and was breathing a stream of lightning. Under

the statue was a thin book. I walked over to
the statue and picked up the book. On the
cover were the words, "Bronze Dragon." I
opened it. It was handwritten.

Bronze Dragon

Congratulations, Pheonix. I was in
the egg you hugged when you were small.
My name is Pherox, and I am the same
type of kinzi as my mother, Kelladine, so
I can change to anything. Also, I am able
to gift kinzi powers to you and your
friend because I made you half-kinzi.
Practice your power to make this world a
better place and to bring hope to the heart
of the hopeless, a smile to the face of the
saddest. I grant you now the power to
change to a Bronze Dragon, my second
shape. You have already discovered my

first shape - a fairy. Here is the information on Bronze Dragons I have found. Use it, as I have said before; use it for the good of others.

Perhaps we shall meet one day. Until then, I will leave you information in books like this one.

Bronze

The Bronze Dragon is one of the most spectacular of Dragon breeds. It has extremely large wings when fully grown and is one of the few dragons who is able to make a relationship with humans.

Breath Weapon (s): Lightning, stinking gasses, fog/mist, and water.

Power (s): Mind reading, telegraphic communication, Breathing underwater, force fields, and bending.

The Bronze Dragon tends to protect good things and humans. It has no Dragonenemy, rather it loathes all evil.

I truly hope you enjoy the Bronze Dragon Shape. Use it well, young friend, use it well.

When I had read the last word, the book and the world around me disappeared and I was in my house, on the couch. My family and Conderen were bending over me with worried faces.

I sat up. "What?" I asked, wondering why they looked so concerned.

"Pheonix......" began Mom.

"You got knocked out!" Finished Conderen dramatically.

"What?! I wasn't knocked out......... I was just somewhere else." Mom and Dad looked at each other worriedly.

"Flowers and a dragon statue," I muttered under my breath as if they would understand.

"Anyway..... Do you like my wings?" I gave them a quick flutter, pushing their hair away from their faces.

Mom looked speechless. Conderen looked ready to laugh. My brother, Bendo, looked relieved. Dad looked slightly annoyed.

"Hey! You can't just fall over unconscious and the next minute wake up and want to show off your wings," protested Dad.

"She has a point," giggled Conderen.

"Just look at the size of them!"

My wings *were* big. Thirteen is a pretty large number - especially when put into feet. The bottom pair were about six feet long.

Mom decided to put aside her concerns. "Pheonix......" she said, as she wrapped her arm around my shoulders, "I think we should call another underground meeting."

I was just fine with that.

"Pheonix, just so you know, you can't just call a meeting so you can talk to friends. The button I pressed sounds an alarm through each house on Timber. Each family than comes to the cave. Only use the alarm if it's for something VERY important. But - I think this is important enough, don't you?"

I nodded.

"Okay, let's go." We walked downstairs and Mom opened the tunnel with the "piece of playdough." We trotted to the cave. As before, there were a few families already there and more were coming in through other tunnels connected to the cave. I had folded up my wings before going into the tunnel, so they were hidden as long as I kept my back out of sight.

Mom took a deep breath.

"Remember the last time I called a meeting?"

Nods.

"Well....." she took another deep breath.

"They've grown."

There were words of astonishment from the people in the cave.

"A lot. Would you like to see them?"

Voices rose.

"She has them folded up behind her. *Would* you like to see them? Raise hands."

All the kids under 13 raised their hands.

"Okay. Anaji, Wilnor, please come forward."

The two Spruces stood up and walked toward me. I smiled at them. Mom told them to go to my back and unfold what they found. She whispered to me not to let them, to keep my wings folded.

At first they just stood at my back, staring. Then they reached out and touched my wings. Wilnor was the first to start tugging gently at my wings, Anaji looked afraid she might hurt me.

After a tiny bit, Anaji started tugging too, and soon they were both tugging vigorously. Soon it felt like they might tear my

31

wings from my back. I winced as Wilnor's fingernails dug into them. After they had made me wince [badly] around ten more times and I was truly afraid they might tear into them, I turned my head toward them and asked them to stop. They still hadn't unfolded them.

Mom asked them to go back to their seats and they obeyed. Then she asked me to spread my wings, though to keep them out of reach of anyone who might want to grab them. I obeyed and unfolded my wings until they filled the cave.

Everyone ooohed, aaaaaahed, or gasped, Except the adults. *They* didn't say anything. They just sat there, stunned, thinking about what they were seeing. (Us kids tend to be the faster thinkers.)

Anaji Spruce tapped my arm. I looked down at her and she asked me, "Can you fly??" I didn't know what to say. I hadn't tried to fly since I jumped out of the apple tree. But I guess I could fly - maybe.

"Pheonix, your -" Mr. Aspen gave a small shudder. "- *Wings* are crowding the place a bit. Maybe we could go outside?"

Everyone agreed, so we carried the meeting outside. I stretched my wings in circles - they had been at an odd angle in the cave.

"I was asked if I could fly a few moments ago," I said, hesitating. "I don't know, but I might be able to. Would anybody like me to try?"

All the kids raised their hands.

There were more kids than grown-ups.

"Okay," I said, "I'll try."

I spread my wings and moved them up and down, as I was always seeing butterflies do. I flipped forward and fell flat on my face.

Swirly, bright colors filled my mind, along with a sound not unlike wind chimes. It took me a bit to figure out what it was - laughter! Pherox, the kinzi, was laughing at me!

Instead of being embarrassed, I started laughing too. Soon everybody else was laughing. Pherox whispered to me, <Do not copy other beings, for you are not like them. Move your wings naturally.> I obeyed and, still giggling, moved my wings as my heart told me to. I flapped harder, and suddenly my feet were no longer on the ground! I froze from surprise and fell flat on my face - again!

Pherox's laughter still rang in my ears as I tried again, (and again, and again.) Finally, I managed to flit above the people's heads before landing on my hands and knees.

Pherox praised me with warm colors and a thrumming sound, like a cat purring, <Good job, my young friend. Good job.>

CHAPTER FIVE

The meeting had ended. We had all gone to our own homes. It was almost noon and I hadn't had breakfast. I was starving! But something told me I should be *outside*, not *inside* at the moment.

Opening the back door, I stepped outside. A steady buzz, like static electricity, was rippling through the air. This I found odd and slightly alarming. But the oddest thing about it was that I could *see* the electricity. It billowed and swirled like Pherox's messages, only its strings and sails glistened with the same rainbow iridescence that was on my wings. As the strands of this electric rainbow twisted and folded, they snapped and crackled, like my wings.

Suddenly a loud SNAP! sounded in my head, making my ears ring, and a whole new realm of possibilities opened up, full of power and flight. I dived in, and suddenly the world began to change. It grew, only a little, but enough to make a noticeable difference. I felt myself changing, my muscles growing stronger, my eyesight sharpening, and my temperature was controlled by my choice. The muscles for my bottom wings disappeared, the shape of the top ones changed. I changed in many other ways, and I ended up like this:

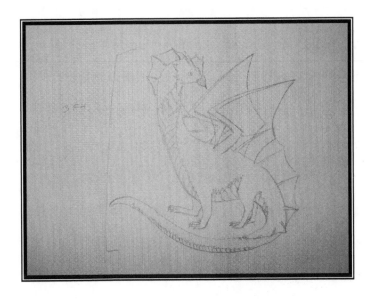

It felt wonderful - I had so much power, I could hardly contain it. I opened my mouth and shot a bolt of lightning into the sky. The rainbows of electricity cleared, leaving me in my own yard, in the shape of a baby Bronze Dragon.

My kinzi powers hadn't left me, and neither had the sense that Pherox was right beside me. I put my claws on the bark of the pine and imagined it disappearing. It did so, and I felt a surge of power surge through me. I grew. My breath weapon, which before had been only lightning, now included water.

I splashed water into my cupped paws and made it into a ball, bending it into a wet sphere. I had yet to master this skill, though, and the sphere splashed to the ground. I suddenly felt as if I was being watched. I spun around, but nothing was there. A piece of rough paper skittered across the ground. I pounced on it, uncurling it with my thin, mobile claws. I read:

Bi wer, ow yung kinzi, fore eye stawc yoo thow yoo downt

si mi. Eye stawc yoo fore deth.
BI WER!!!

I frowned at the bad spelling, admiring the beautiful calligraphy. The words puzzled me, though.

Why would *anyone* "stawc" me "fore deth"?! I was not afraid, only deeply puzzled. Suddenly I flipped the paper over. What I saw chilled me to the bones: the sign of a Black Dragon, a blot of blood. I was filled with anger. I would have been frightened to my very heart in human form, but the feelings a dragon has for its enemy are very powerful.

But to defeat this Black Dragon, I must gather information. I imagined a paper with facts about Black Dragons in it and held out my paws. A black, leather-bound thin book dropped into them. On it, in gold letters, were the words:

Black Dragons

I shifted into my human form, and, feeling a fear not good to explain, looked around cautiously and opened the book. The startlingly evil picture on the first page took my breath away. It was such a life-like illustration that it looked as if it might jump out of the book and devour me in one bite.

I slammed the book shut and tried to concentrate above the din of my pounding heart.

<Pherox!> I called telegraphically once I had changed back into a Bronze Dragon. <Where are you?!>

<I'm right next to you>, I heard. I whipped around, but did not see anything. Suddenly a blade of grass next to my bare foot

quivered and started to change. It grew and pulsed, then it split open to reveal a half-grown Bronze Dragon, like myself, only bigger, with longer, sharper horns, simply immense wings and a more impressive frill.

I stared at Pherox, not sure what to say. The kinzi stared back down at me with unblinking, molten-gold eyes. I asked her,

<How did you grow so advanced????>

She sent her wind-chime laugh through me and lowered her head until it was level with mine.

<Well, my young friend, there are more jobs for my powers in my world. And -> she looked into space, contemplating. <- we kinzies are more common, more appreciated *there* than we are *here*.>

<Oh......... um, Pherox?>

<Yes?>

<Can I bring Conderen out here?>

<Of course, my young friend> said Pherox,
golden squiggles lacing her voice.

<She is my sister.>

My mouth popped open and hung there.

<Sister?!?>

<Yes, as are you.> A warm, red-gold smile
danced its way through my head. I rushed into
the house, not remembering to change shape.
When I came across Mom, she stared down at
me and fell over backwards. The loud *thump!*
Brought the rest of the family - and Conderen -
running. Dad kicked me and yelped. His bare
foot glanced off my armor-like scales and he
hopped away on one foot. Bendo took a quick
look into my eyes and smiled, as did Conderen. I
then realized why my parents had acted so

strange and shifted hurriedly back into a human.

I walked over to Mom, who had cautiously propped herself up on one elbow. She hadn't been unconscious, only playing dead - I had sensed that when she had fallen over.

"Sorry,"

I told her, sounding as truly apologetic as I could. She had seen me change, I had felt her eyes on me.

"Conderen, I'd like it if you came outside, there's something I want you to see." Conderen followed me outside, gasping as she saw the magnificent form of the Bronze in our backyard. She ran to meet her sister, who changed to fairy-form and met the embrace. The air crackled and fizzed around them, turning a dark gray color. But this electricity, I sensed, did not signify a coming power. I held out my paws, trying to bend the rainbow lightning away from them, back to no avail.

A tendril of the lightning came out from around them and snapped, sending me flying. Angrily, I let out a stream of my own lightning at it. Instead of withering from my power, a sheath of black, scale-like stuff fell away from it and as it merged with my lightning, bringing it back to the other strands, it turned rainbow-colored and uncurled happily from the two fairies. This happened so fast that I hadn't even landed from my whack yet.

<Well done, young friend>

I heard and suddenly everything around me shrank significantly. The tiny, almost shriveled wings on my back snapped open, catching me before I hit the ground, and my hearing sharpened like a knife. I heard sounds from almost 1,000 miles away, among this flood of sounds I heard my friend, Anaji's voice. She sounded frightened. Tuning in on it, I heard Anaji Spruce yelling for help.

Chapter six

Black Dragons

A most evil specimen, this dragon may be hiding right below your nose! It may attack you when you think there is nothing to harm you, for it can turn invisible.

Breath Weapon (s): Poison gas, oil, explosive gas, black fire

Power(s): paralyzing liquid-filled claws, mirages, black-firebending, turning invisible, making an object or creature do its will (not effective on some creatures, and undone by a Bronze Dragon's Lightning.)

The Black Dragon tends to be a traitor to all who are unfortunate enough to believe its words. The Black Dragon's Dragonenemy (s) are all good dragons.

I read these words from the Black Dragon book as I flew over the trees toward Anaji's cries. I was going at quite a speed, but not fast enough, I felt. After making the book disappear, I imagined a large maple tree disappearing, and felt myself speed up as it gave me power. I than imagined a huge redwood in its place, and sped up even more.

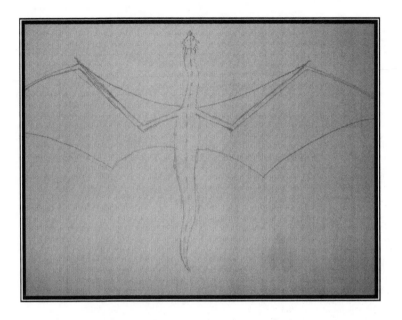

I used my power at large-scale as I flew, speeding me up, making me more advanced and gaining breath weapons and Bronze powers.

By the time I got to where Anaji's voice was coming from, I was a full-fledged Bronze Dragon. I flew through thick fog and almost crashed into a huge rock wall.

Folding my wings, I dove toward the ground and almost tore down a large cluster of huge pine trees. I spread my wings with a thundering bang and flapped them furiously, propelling me at top-speed towards Anaji's voice.

I almost passed her, but clung to the rock wall. Oddly enough, the voice was coming from the wall. Suddenly, the air took on a menacing chill. I sensed my enemy, evil, in the form of the Black Dragon nearby.

I half-spread my massive, streamlined wings and a force field appeared at the tips, spreading until there was a huge, glimmering force field around my whole body.

And none too soon - at the instant the force field was completed, a humongous weight slammed into the shield, driving it into the granite face. Anaji's voice stopped abruptly, as if it had been sucked out of her. As the Black slammed into my force field, it was shocked into reappearing.

It was a horrible dull black monster with forward-curled, barbed horns sprouting from behind its thin, sharp ears. Its brown-black claws were as pointed as needles, except they curled slightly inward.

An extremely long tail with a sickle-shaped barb at the end twisted and writhed below it. Its blackish, neon-green eyes flashed angrily from under jagged eye ridges and its spiny, thin, black wings filtered the sunlight into a dull, brown-black as it fell upon me. It seemed piteous, almost trapped though, despite its ferocious looks.

The Black turned and flew back about fifty feet, only to turn around and fly toward me at an amazing speed. I pulled down my force field, dodged the attack, and pulled up the force field quite easily. I was testing my opponent's abilities, a talent that came naturally to my dragon form.

I had found so far that this dragon was very powerful, but hardly agile.

Not forgetting what I was here for, I edged away from the stone where Anaji's voice had come from, so as not to cave in the rock around her.

The Black turned again on me, leveling its head to aim its forward-pointing horns at me. I crackled a bolt of lightning in my throat as a warning, letting some spark in the dragon's direction; but instead of striking the dragon, the lightning hit the inside of my force field and bounced back at me, hitting my armor-like scales and passing through them. I started, more surprised with the lightning's reaction to the force field than the physical shock the lightning gave me - it merely snapped back into me with a fizzing feeling, bouncing back to the place it had come from.

The Black was charging again now, hurtling through the air like a locomotive. I dodged it again, and it buried its long horns in the rock behind where I had been. I still had my force field around me, and shed it so I could use my breath weapon on the Black.

The Black pressed its paw to the rock, freeing its stuck horns. We faced each other in the air, two immensely powerful creatures about to charge. I readied a crackling bolt in my throat, ready to consume my opponent as it charged. The Black bobbed its head and a green fog seeped out of its mouth, rising in snaking tendrils in my direction. I took a deep breath and held it. (This came naturally since Bronze dragons often make the main entrances to their lairs underwater tunnels.)

The Black drew its head up and back, readying its poisonous gas in its throat. The lightning in my own crackled and snapped loudly in my ears, as if wanting to leave my throat and swallow the Black in a coat of thick, pure lightning.

The Black's breath weapon left its mouth in a thick, noxious green sheet. It seemed to make its way through the air in super-slow motion, and I quickly exhaled the lightning and ducked under the gas to suck in another breath. I watched the lightning glide through the air toward the Black's chest with the super-slow vision I had gained. The Black watched the lightning snap toward its chest. It tried to dodge, but was too slow. My bolt hit the right-hand side of its chest, sending it sprawling. The Black plummeted to the ground as my slow motion vision gained pace to normal.

To my surprise, a dull black, almost brown film fell off the dragon as it fell toward the trees almost a mile below. My hate toward the dragon disappeared, rather turning to the scale-like film that had fallen from the dragon that, as it floated slowly to the ground, was evaporating into nothingness.

I had the sudden urge to save the paralyzed Black and I flew on my huge wings to catch it. The dragon was lighter than I, in fact, it seemed almost starved. I gained on it in no time and fell under it for a second before hovering with the dragon on my back. I landed gently on the ground, and, not forgetting my friend, raced back up the cliff face.

The mist had cleared, and I quickly spotted the crumbled rock where the Black had crushed my force field into the mottled gray stone. I flew to it and clung to the rock face, wondering how I should continue. I lifted a golden claw and dug it into the rock, which gave way easily when I applied pressure.

I began digging through the rock.

I dug a tunnel the length of my dragon body before the wall in front of me began to collapse. I lay my paw flat against the stone and pushed on it. It crumbled before my strength and I stepped into a cave hardly able to contain my form. I placed my paw against the wall and imagined the cave growing bigger.

It did so, and only then did a notice the fainted figure of my friend, Anaji, crumpled against the far wall. No wonder - I had not yet made it known that I was her friend, Pheonix. To tell the truth, I hardly missed my human form - the power of a Bronze Dragon was wonderful, but I knew that, so as not to harm my friend with my sharp claws and powerful strength, I would have to switch back.

I changed to the normal, ex-average girl with wings to carry Anaji to my tunnel. I placed my hand on her cheek and imagined her to be awake. Immediately this was true. Anaji blinked and sat up, surprised, with an almost frightened shine in her eye.

She hugged me, saying,

"Oh Pheonix! I'm so glad you came!"

Then,

"But..... Black Diamond will be here soon. Where will you hide?" Then,

"Oh, Pheonix! I heard another dragon, with Diamond. It was scary - I called for help when Diamond left, but then I heard the rock rumble and I stopped. I was SO scared!"

Anaji pummeled me with questions before I was finally able to get a word in myself.

"Anaji..." I said, hesitating.

"Anaji, to get you home, I have to do something scary. I was the other dragon. I can turn into a Bronze Dragon, which is a type of good dragon. You'll have to ride on my back for me to get you down from here. Please don't be scared. I'll get you home."

Anaji's eyes were wide with surprise, but I could tell that she was not as frightened as she thought she was.

"Okay," she said hesitantly.

Soon I was flying back toward my home with Anaji on my back. Minutes later, we arrived in - well, I had to clear some trees - my yard. I let Anaji slide down my leg and changed back to Pheonix, as everybody else knew me.

*   *   *   *   *

When everybody was gathered under my mother's call, I was announced a hero for saving Anaji Spruce. Black Diamond was introduced once I learned that she was the only good Black Dragon left in this world - that is why her scales sparkled in the sun and her eyes danced with the blue spark of Life which all on His side have in their hearts.

Back at my home, I opened my huge Bronze' wings and glided swiftly above the trees. I didn't have to be this way if I didn't want to, but I had learned the good in being different.

That's just the way I am.

Still, I wonder about the Black who was controlling Black Diamond when she attacked me.

About THE STORYTeller

The Bible says that good will ultimately rise above evil. This story explains that with a taste of adventure.

I am 11 years old, live in a town called Ann Arbor and wish I lived in the same place as Pheonix, the girl in my story. The part where she makes her room look like a forest is based off of my dream room.

I wish I could have more pets, but (here in Michigan.) I only own a dwarf hamster named Bear. He's super cute, and if I become famous one day, no doubt he'll get his own fan mail.

If you liked *Me, With Wings*, then I'm sure you will like the next book in the *Wings* trilogy: *Wings at Leisure.*

By the way, I love meeting new friends so please contact me by email: pheonix.stories@gmail.com.

Thank you, and God Bless!

Write to the author directly at
pheonix.stories@gmail.com
Or mail your letter to:
Pheonix Stories
PO Box 131374
Ann Arbor, MI 48113

Made in the USA
Charleston, SC
20 September 2012